SPACE
Ever since she was young,
little Nova has always
wanted to go to the moon.

Nova's parents always told her anything you set your mind on, you can do it.

Nova was not going
to let anything or anyone stop her.

Nova was excited,
but she knew she would need
a spaceship to get to the moon.

Building that spaceship would require some help. So she went to her big brother Max.

Max had been playing video games for hours when he suddenly heard a knock at his door.

Max answered the door and saw Nova staring back at him with a huge smile on her face.

What do you want?
I need your help to build a spaceship to go to the moon.

Max laughed at Nova as he replied,
"You'll never get to the moon, you
nerd, that's impossible."

MAX
Nova wasn't going to let Max stop her from getting to the moon, so she went to go ask her friend Emily for help.

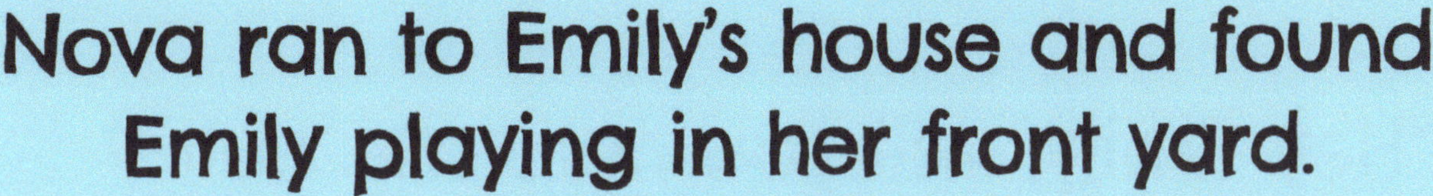

Nova ran to Emily's house and found Emily playing in her front yard.

"Hey Emily, will you help me build a spaceship to go to the moon?" Nova asked.

Emily replied excitedly, "Yes! I want to help you get to the moon." So the two friends set off on their new adventure.

They would need all the materials they could find, so Nova went to the only place she knew had all the supplies she needed... her dad's garage.

In the garage Nova and Emily found some cardboard boxes, an old trash can, and some tools they would need to build their spaceship.

They loaded their supplies in a red wagon and brought them to the backyard to begin working on the spaceship.

It took almost 2 hours to build their spaceship, but it was finally complete. They were finally ready for take off!

Nova climbed into the pilot's seat of the spaceship and gave the signal to Emily to start the countdown.

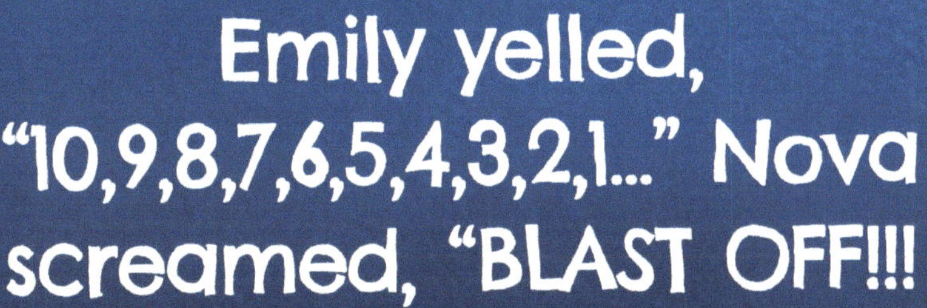

Emily yelled,
"10,9,8,7,6,5,4,3,2,1..." Nova
screamed, "BLAST OFF!!!

The spaceship started to rattle as it started to lift off. Before they knew it, they were in space.. next stop, the moon.

They saw the moon
getting closer as they
looked out to see a tiny little
Earth in the distance.

When Nova and Emily landed on the moon, they happily jumped up and down screaming "We made it!"

Nova was happy to have a
friend like Emily. She was also
happy she proved Max wrong.

The two friends then began to look around and explore the moon when they noticed a mysterious figure in the shadows... TO BE CONTINUED

www.ingramcontent.com/pod-product-compliance
Ingram Content Group UK Ltd.
Pitfield, Milton Keynes, MK11 3LW, UK
UKHW060115300726
14090UKWH00002B/209
* 9 7 9 8 7 8 5 0 2 9 2 4 8 *